Happy Birthday, Dear Dragon

A Follett JUST Beginning-To-Read book

Happy Birthday, Dear Dragon

Margaret Hillert

Illustrated by Carl Kock

FOLLETT PUBLISHING COMPANY
Chicago

International Standard Book Number: 0-695-40743-0 Titan binding

International Standard Book Number: 0-695-30743-6 Paper binding

23456789/81807978

This looks good, Mother.
What a big one.
Oh, this is fun.

Here is something.
What is it?
I can not guess.

Oh, look here.
Look at this
   —and this
   —and this!

And here is something that can jump up.

Now come with me.
I want to get you something.
Run, run, run.

10

Here we go.
In here. In here.
We will look at the dogs.

But we have a dog, Father.
I like the one we have.
I do not want this dog.

Here is something little.
Do you want this?
You can look at it.
It can look at you.

No, I do not like it.
What can it do?
It can not play with me.

Look down here.
You can have this one.
Do you like it?
See it jump.

I like that little one.
But it is not what I want.
Come away.
Come away.

Here is what I want.

Oh, will you get it for me?

I like it.

I like it.

I like it!

Come with me.
Come to my house.
I like you.
We can have fun.

20

Look, Mother.
See what I have.
It can play with me.

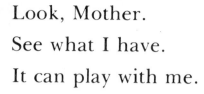

I see. I see.

It is funny.

We will find something for it.

I want to go for a ride.
I will get in.
Help me.
Help me.

Here we go.
Run, run, run.
What fun.
What fun.

Will you do something for me?
Will you help me with this?

Now, *you* have one.

Have two.

Have three.

You are a big help.

Oh, my. Oh, my.
Look what you can do.
I like this.

Here you are with me.
And here I am with you.
Oh, what a happy birthday, dear dragon.

Happy Birthday, Dear Dragon

Uses of This Book: Reading for fun. This easy-to-read story about a delightful pet is sure to excite the rich imaginations of children.

Word List

All of the 64 words used in *Happy Birthday, Dear Dragon* are listed. Regular verb forms and plurals of words already on the list are not listed separately, but the endings are given in parentheses after the word.

1	happy		it		you		see
	birthday		I		run	**18**	away
	dear		can	**12**	we	**19**	for
	dragon		not		go	**20**	my
5	this		guess		in		house
	look(s)	**7**	at		will	**23**	funny
	good		and		the		find
	mother	**8**	that		dog(s)	**24**	ride
	what		jump	**14**	but		help
	a		up		have	**27**	two
	big	**10**	now		father		three
	one		come		like		are
	oh		with		do	**31**	am
	is		me	**15**	little		
	fun		want	**16**	no		
6	here		to		play		
	something		get	**17**	down